LOUISE LOVES ART

For Maggie, my masterpiece

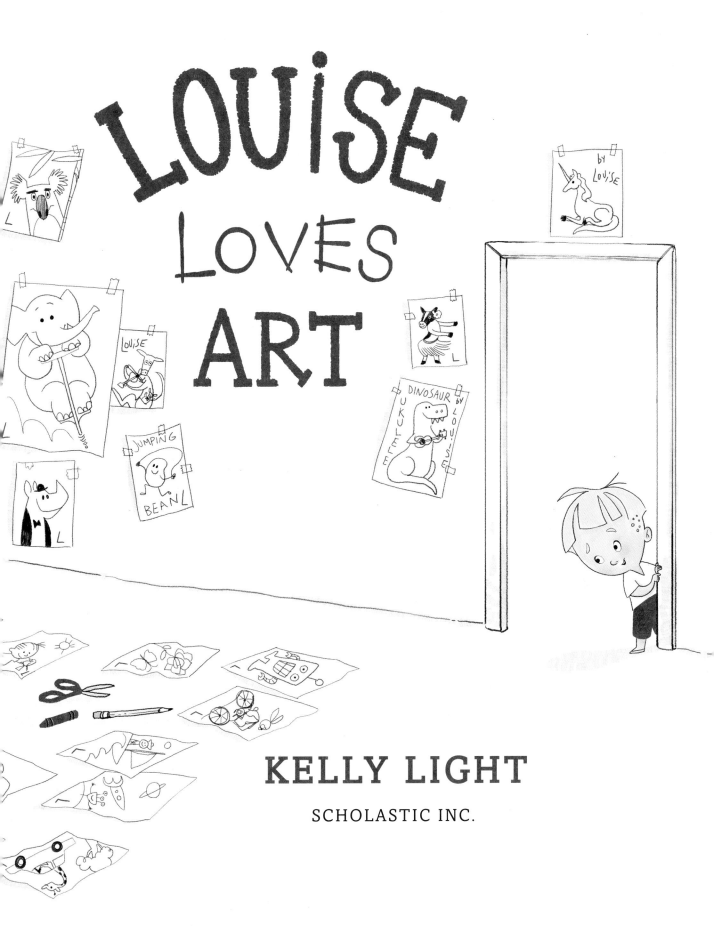

LOUISE LOVES ART

KELLY LIGHT

SCHOLASTIC INC.

I love art!
It's my imagination on the outside.

So little time, so much to draw.
One of these drawings will be my masterpiece—
the greatest drawing I have ever done!

To be a great artist, you have to notice everything.

Every line . . .

every curve . . .

Wait—hold that pose! I will capture your cat-ness!

I've done it.
So fierce! So feline! So fantastic . . .
a masterpiece!

Louise?

Not now, Art. I have to get ready for my show.

PORTRAIT OF A YOUNG ARTISTE

I have to hang each picture just so. . . .

LOUISE

Louise?

It's my pièce de résistance!
I know the perfect spot for it.

The Gallery du Fridge!

LOUISE!

AHHH!

ART!

How could you?

It's my drawing . . .

my masterpiece!

Sorry.

Oh, Art. I love it.

It's your masterpiece.
And I know the perfect spot for it.

Voilà!

ISBN 978-0-545-88788-5

Copyright © 2014 by Kelly Light. All rights reserved.
Published by Scholastic Inc., 557 Broadway, New York, NY 10012,
by arrangement with Balzer + Bray, an imprint of HarperCollins Children's Books,
a division of HarperCollins Publishers. SCHOLASTIC and associated
logos are trademarks and/or registered trademarks of Scholastic Inc.

13 12 13 10 9 8 7 6 5 4 3 2   16 17 18 19 20 21/0

Printed in the U.S.A.   08

First Scholastic printing, September 2015

The artist used many black Prismacolor pencils and Photoshop to create the illustrations for this book.
Typography by Alison Donalty